Dragonfly Ministries

A Walk With Papa

Written by Patty Zemanick
Illustrated by Sandra Hammack

This book is dedicated to God... the true author of this story; to my beloved children Lindsey and Ryan, to my parents and the Zemanick family. Thank you Mary, Martha and Dragonfly Ministries for sharing the vision and Sam for bringing these pages to life.

Patty Zemanick, Author

I am thankful to God for granting me the opportunity to illustrate the story He led Patty to write. Special thanks to Mary, Martha, and Dragonfly Ministries for believing in and dedicating many hours to the publishing of this book. Loving thanks to my husband Thomas for his unending devotion, my children Rachael and Seth, and sister Mary, for their love and encouragement. And in loving memory of Dad for his unconditional love, whose images can be seen in these pages. May this book bless you who read it so that you will share its story of Christ with those you cherish.

Sandra Hammack
Illustrator

© 2006 by Patty Zemanick
Illustrated by Sandra Hammack
All rights reserved.
Printed in China
Published by Dragonfly Ministries Publishers
Plano, Texas

ISBN 978-0-9788289-0-5

Papa took me by the hand and said, "Let's take a walk."
He opened up the door, then began to talk ...
He said, "I've been watching you. You're growing like a weed.
It's finally time I showed you where this old path will lead."

1

We headed down a twisted path which led to a field of hay.
I rolled across the ground while Papa watched me play.
I gathered up some hay and made a little bed.
Papa gave me his jacket – a pillow for my head.

Soon we were walking again and the field was far behind.
But the brush became so thick, the path we could hardly find.

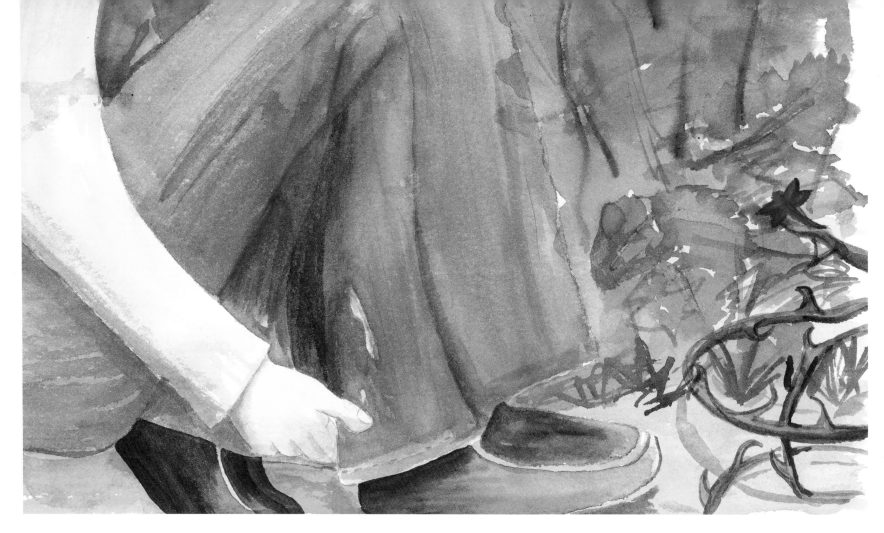

"Ouch" – my leg got scratched. I looked and saw a thorn.
Papa lifted me up, but my jeans were already torn.
Papa looked at my leg and said, "It will be okay.
The scratch is pretty small; soon it will go away."

He gently put me down and we were walking once again.
We were going to a place where I had never been.
It was a deep, dark forest with trees that reached the sky.
The smell of moss was in the air. I touched ferns as we walked by.

Some branches had fallen across the path, I tried to push them aside.
Suddenly, a twig went snap! When it struck my back I cried.
Papa gathered me in his arms. I looked at his eyes so blue.
He knew that I was hurting cause there were tears in his eyes too.

There we sat beneath an oak. Papa hugged me for a while.
Then he gave me a wink. His wrinkles made me smile.
Back on our feet once again, I heard sounds of a stream.
I ran along the path. It looked just like a dream.

Water rushing over rocks – some places it just trickled.
I put my feet into the stream. It was so cold it tickled.

Just then a piece of twisted wood, looking like a cross,
floated past my feet and stopped along the moss.

Taking the cross into my hands, I ran to Papa's side.
He said, "This is a treasure" as he looked at it with pride.

I put the cross away and asked, "Where will this trail end?"
Papa said, "Be patient child, it's just around the bend."

From the distance I could see a clearing up ahead.
I ran as quickly as I could. Where had this old path led?
I stepped into the clearing. We were on a tall, tall hill.
I could see for miles around. The world seemed quiet and still.

"I come here often," Papa said. "This is where I like to pray.
I sit and talk with God. He hears every word I say."

Papa said, "Now child — come here and chat with me.
As we walked along the path, what did your young eyes see?"
I thought about our walk and the places we had been.
I thought for quite a while, then finally answered him.

14

"I saw a field of hay where I made a bed.
You remember, don't you?" and Papa shook his head.
"Yes, I remember. I watched you run and play.
Can you think of another child who also slept on hay?"

15

"Baby Jesus did," I said, "on that special night.
They laid Him in a manger beneath a star so bright."

"What happened next?" Papa asked.
I said, "The bushes and the thorn.
Look, here's my scratch
and where my jeans were torn."

17

"I see your scratch," said Papa. "You know, Jesus suffered too.
A crown of thorns they placed on His head. He was hurting, much like you."
Then the soldiers laughed and said "Come see the King of Jews."
They tore His clothes while shouting, "Your life you'll surely lose."

"Remember in the forest, when you pushed the twigs aside?
The soldiers hurt His back like that, and like you, I'm sure He cried."
"Papa, why did they hurt our Jesus? Was He being bad?"
"No my child, He was perfect. But our sins made God real sad."

19

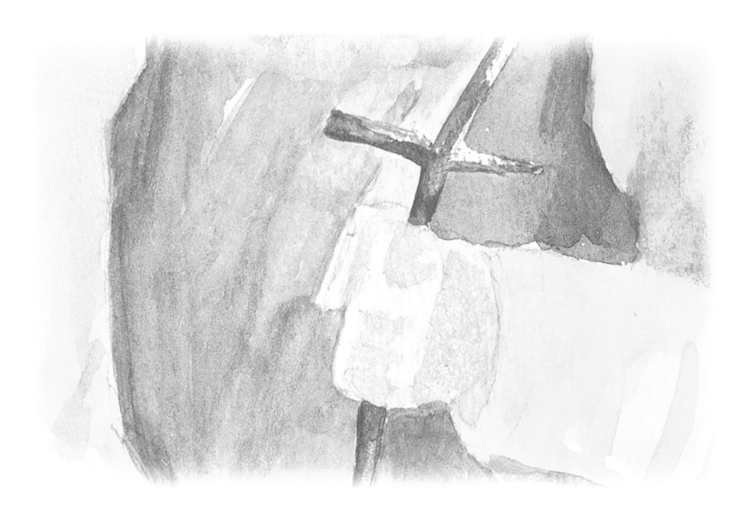

Papa said, "Where is that cross you found floating in the stream?
Let's look at it once more and I'll tell you what I mean."

"God looked down from heaven and everywhere He saw
the sin in people's hearts as they disobeyed His law.
God knew we were not perfect, so there had to be a way
to erase the wrong we did each and every day."

"That's why He gave us Jesus to die upon the cross.
His death erased our sins so our souls would not be lost.
But death wasn't strong enough to keep Him in His grave,
because three days later He rose again! Despite sin, we are saved!"

"If Jesus lives inside your heart, then someday when you die
God will bring you home to His kingdom in the sky!"
"Is Jesus in my heart?" I asked. "Does He live there now?
I want to invite Him in. Can you show me how?"
"Oh, my precious child – that's why I brought you here.
I've shared this path and place with you, to make God's message clear."

Then Papa took me by the hand — but not to take a walk.
This time we knelt down on the grass as he began to talk.

24

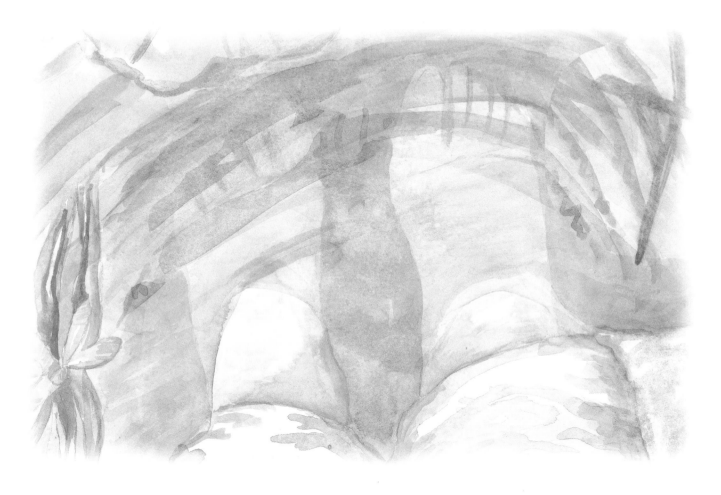

"If you want Jesus in your heart, just invite Him in.
Tell Jesus how much you love Him and ask forgiveness for your sins."

I prayed …

"Jesus – I do love you. Please come into my heart.
Forgive me for my sins. From you, I'll never part."

We headed back toward home – With Jesus, my new friend.
I couldn't help but smile, "cause He's with me til" ...

The End

FOR ETERNITY!

Isaiah 7:14

Therefore the Lord himself will give you a sign: the virgin will be with child and will give birth to a son, and will call Him Immanuel."

Matthew 1:20-22

An angel of the Lord appeared to him in a dream and said, "Joseph son of David, do not be afraid to take Mary home as your wife, because what is conceived in her is from the Holy Spirit. She will give birth to a son, and you are to give him the name Jesus, because he will save his people from their sins." All this took place to fulfill what the Lord had said through the prophet: "The virgin will be with child and will give birth to a son, and they will call him Immanuel —which means, God with us."

Luke 2:4

So Joseph also went up from the town of Nazareth in Galilee to Judea, to Bethlehem the town of David, because he belonged to the house and line of David. He went there to register with Mary, who was pledged to be married to him and was expecting a child. While they were there, the time came for the baby to be born, and she gave birth to her firstborn, a son. She wrapped him in cloths and placed him in a manger, because there was no room for them in the inn.

Luke 2: 21

On the eighth day, when it was time to circumcise him, he was named Jesus, the name the angel had given him before he had been conceived.

Matthew 9:35

Then Jesus went about all the cities and villages teaching in their synagogues, preaching the gospel of the kingdom, and healing every sickness and every disease among the people.

Romans 3:23

For all have sinned and fall short of the glory of God.

John 3:17

For God did not send his Son into the world to condemn the world, but to save the world through him.

Matthew 27

Then the governor's soldiers took Jesus into the Praetorium and gathered the whole company of soldiers around him. They stripped him and put a scarlet robe on him, and then twisted together a crown of thorns and set it on his head. They put a staff in his right hand and knelt in front of him and mocked him. "Hail, king of the Jews!" they said. They spit on him, and took the staff and struck him on the head again and again. After they had mocked him, they took off the robe and put his own clothes on him. Then they led him away to crucify him.

Matthew 27:35-44
When they had crucified him, they divided up his clothes by casting lots. And sitting down, they kept watch over him there. Above his head they placed the written charge against him: THIS IS JESUS, THE KING OF THE JEWS. Two robbers were crucified with him, one on his right and one on his left. Those who passed by hurled insults at him, shaking their heads and saying, "You who are going to destroy the temple and build it in three days, save yourself! Come down from the cross, if you are the Son of God!"

In the same way the chief priests, the teachers of the law and the elders mocked him. "He saved others, they said, but he can't save himself!" He's the King of Israel! Let him come down now from the cross, and we will believe in him. He trusts in God. Let God rescue him now if he wants him, for he said, "I am the Son of God." In the same way the robbers who were crucified with him also heaped insults on him.

Matthew 27:50
And when Jesus had cried out again in a loud voice, he gave up his spirit.

Matthew 28:5-10
The angel said to the women, "Do not be afraid, for I know that you are looking for Jesus, who was crucified. He is not here; he has risen, just as he said. Come and see the place where he lay. Then go quickly and tell his disciples: He has risen from the dead and is going ahead of you into Galilee. There you will see him. Now I have told you." So the women hurried away from the tomb, afraid yet filled with joy, and ran to tell his disciples. Suddenly Jesus met them. "Greetings," he said. They came to him, clasped his feet and worshiped him. Then Jesus said to them, "Do not be afraid. Go and tell my brothers to go to Galilee; there they will see me."

Ephesians 1:7
In Jesus, we have redemption through his blood, the forgiveness of sins.

John 3:16
For God so loved the world that he gave his one and only Son, that whoever believes in him shall not perish but have eternal life. For God did not send his Son into the world to condemn the world, but to save the world through him.

John 14:6
Jesus said, "I am the way, the truth and the life, no one comes to the Father except through me."

Dragonfly Ministries